Potty time

Fiona Watt

pictures by Rachel Wells

managing designer: Mary Cartwright   series editor: Jenny Tyler

Bunny and Fido don't wear diapers.

I don't want to wear one.

Diapers get in the way.

Diapers get soggy...

... and smelly.

What's this?

And what's it for?

We can make sandcastles with it.

We can fill it with things.

It makes a good boat for Bunny too.

Ah! If Bunny
can sit on it...